WHO

HAS A

BELLY BUTTON?

To Carly,
My adorable great niece,
May you always be fearless and speak your own mind.
—M. B.

This is for my wonderful mother, Edna.
Thank you for everything!
—H. B.

Special thanks to Barbara French, conservation officer and information specialist for
Bat Conservation International; Dr. Jim Oosterhuis, principal veterinarian, San Diego Wild Animal Park;
and Richard Sears, director of Mingan Island Cetacean Study, Inc.

Published by
PEACHTREE PUBLISHERS, LTD.
1700 Chattahoochee Avenue
Atlanta, Georgia 30318-2112

www.peachtree-online.com

Text © 2004 by Mary Batten
Illustrations © 2004 by Higgins Bond

Illustrations painted in acrylic on cold press illustration board
Text typeset in Baskerville Infant and titles in Univers 75 Black
Manufactured in China

10 9 8 7 6 5 4 3 2 1
First Edition

Library of Congress Cataloging-in-Publication Data

Batten, Mary.
Who has a belly button? / written by Mary Batten ; illustrated by
Higgins Bond.-- 1st ed.
p. cm.
Summary: Introduces what belly buttons are, how they are formed, and how
they differ on the people and animals who have them.
ISBN 1-56145-235-1
1. Navel--Juvenile literature. [1. Belly button. 2. Pregnancy. 3.
Mammals.] I. Bond, Higgins, ill. II. Title.
QM543 .B38 2003
612.6'3--dc21
                                          2003001458

WHO HAS A BELLY BUTTON?

Written by
Mary Batten

Illustrated by
Higgins Bond

Ω
PEACHTREE
ATLANTA

Who has a belly button?
I do. You do.

Cats, dogs, and rabbits do.

But birds, fish, and crabs don't.

Every person in the world has a belly button. So do many animals. Do you know why?

It is because they are *mammals*.

Many animal babies hatch from eggs laid by their mothers, but mammal babies grow inside their mothers until they are ready to be born alive.

All mammal babies drink milk made by their mother's *mammary glands*. The name mammal comes from these mammary glands. Each mammal mother produces milk that is just right for her own baby to drink.

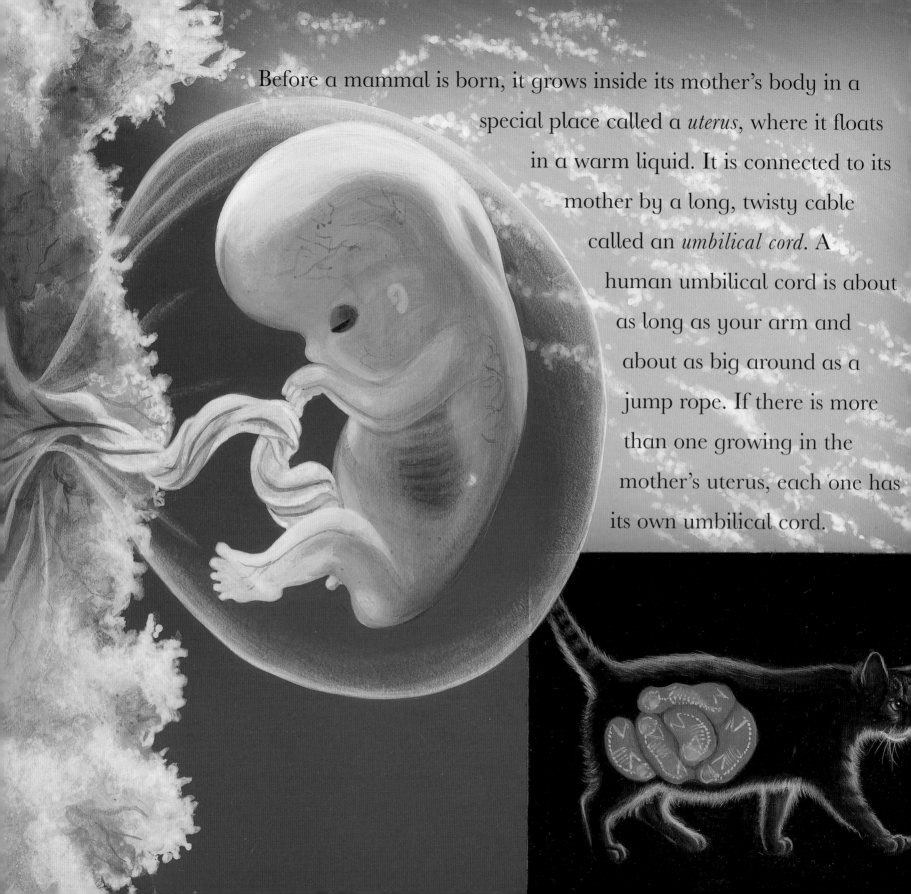

Before a mammal is born, it grows inside its mother's body in a special place called a *uterus*, where it floats in a warm liquid. It is connected to its mother by a long, twisty cable called an *umbilical cord*. A human umbilical cord is about as long as your arm and about as big around as a jump rope. If there is more than one growing in the mother's uterus, each one has its own umbilical cord.

An astronaut is connected to a spaceship by a long cable. This cable is the astronaut's lifeline. It supplies him with *oxygen* to breathe. The baby's umbilical cord is another kind of lifeline.

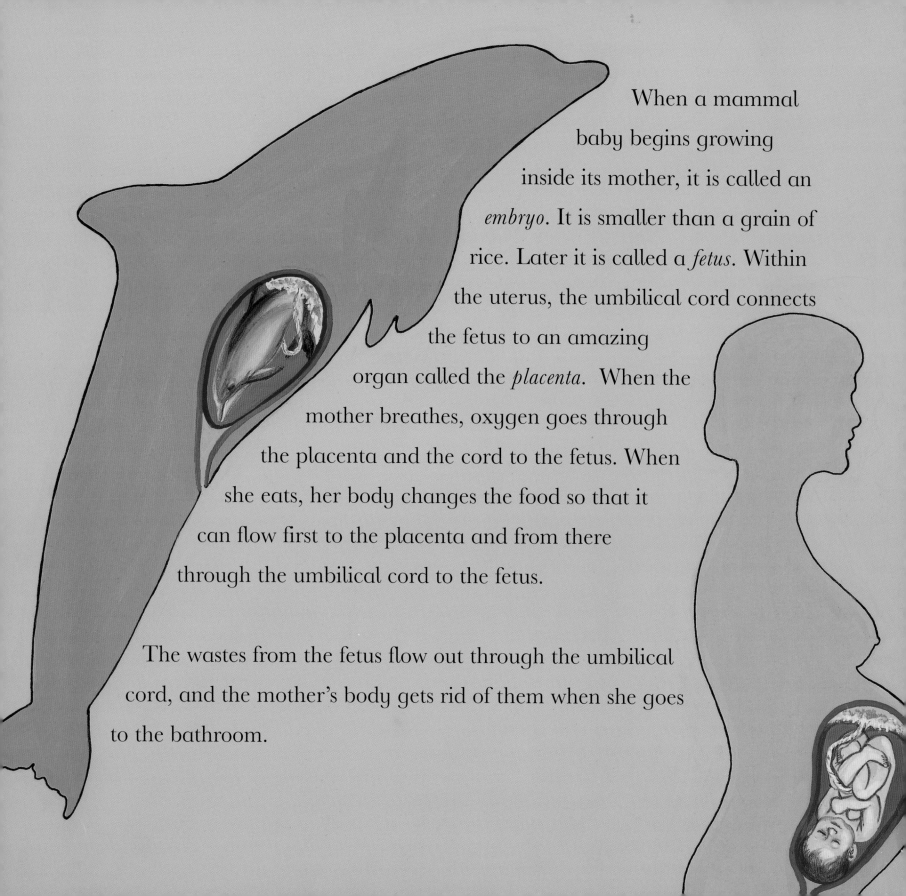

When a mammal baby begins growing inside its mother, it is called an *embryo*. It is smaller than a grain of rice. Later it is called a *fetus*. Within the uterus, the umbilical cord connects the fetus to an amazing organ called the *placenta*. When the mother breathes, oxygen goes through the placenta and the cord to the fetus. When she eats, her body changes the food so that it can flow first to the placenta and from there through the umbilical cord to the fetus.

The wastes from the fetus flow out through the umbilical cord, and the mother's body gets rid of them when she goes to the bathroom.

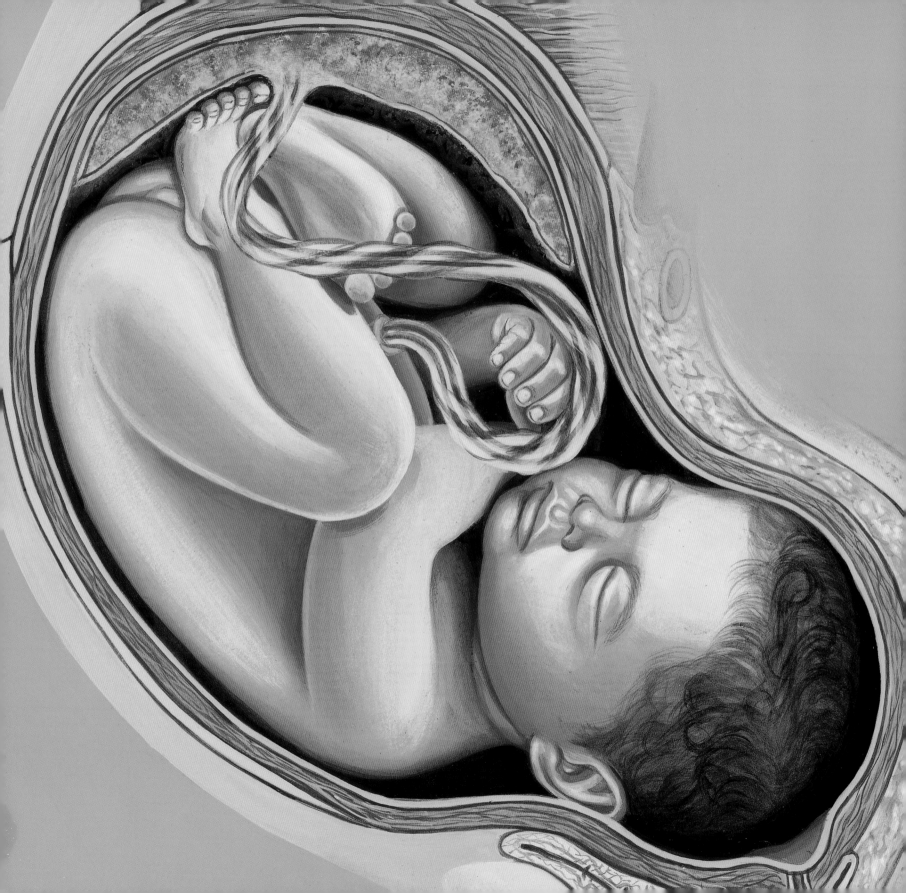

Some mammals take a short time to grow in their mother's uterus. A kitten takes about two months. A human baby grows inside its mother for nine months. Other mammals take longer to develop before birth. A dolphin takes eleven months. An African elephant takes longer than any other mammal on land—twenty-two months—almost two years!

A mammal baby is born when it is able to live outside its mother's body.

After a mammal baby is born, it no longer needs its umbilical cord. The cord must be cut away. This does not hurt the baby or the mother. The stem of the cord forms a hard scab that dries and falls off, leaving a spot called a *navel*. Most of us call it a belly button.

Your belly button is the place where you were connected to your mother—the place where your umbilical cord used to be.

Almost all mammals have belly buttons, but not all of them are as easy to see as ours.

When a puppy or a kitten is born, the umbilical cord breaks off, or the mother animal bites it off. As the animal grows, the belly button is covered by fur.

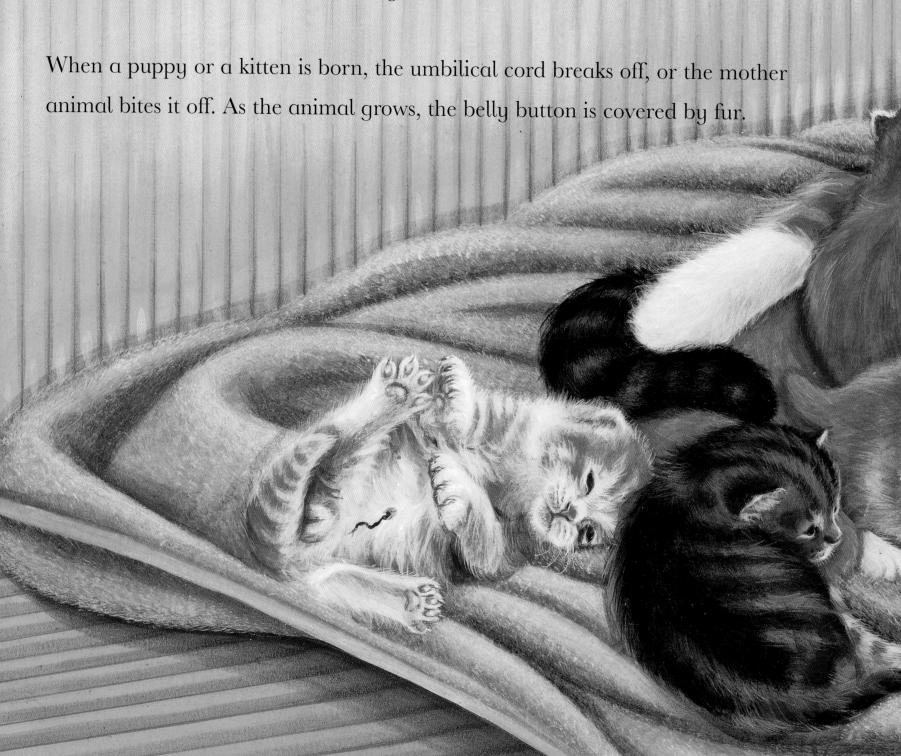

There are about four thousand kinds of mammals.

The largest adult mammal is the blue whale,
which weighs as much as a jet airplane.

The smallest is the bumblebee bat,
which weighs no more than a penny and
is tiny enough to fit in a walnut shell.

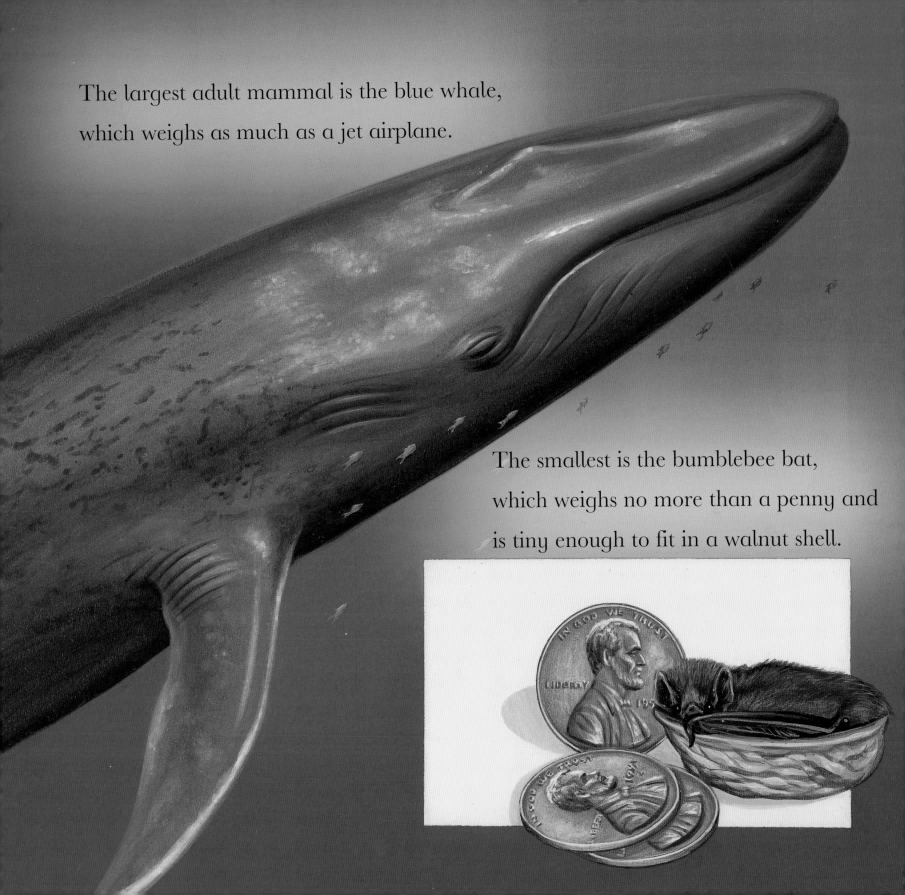

Bats are flying mammals.

When the red bat mother gives birth, she hangs from her tree roost by her feet and thumbs, making a hammock with her body for her baby. Soon after it is born, the baby bat's cord stub falls off, and its belly button is visible for only a short time. Within a few weeks, it is covered by fur.

The blue whale is the largest animal that ever lived on Earth. A newborn baby blue whale is about as long as a school bus and weighs as much as a full-grown rhinoceros! It drinks fifty gallons of its mother's milk a day and gains ten pounds an hour.

The blue whale has the biggest belly button of any animal. It is not round like yours, but more like a furrow about a foot long and eight to twelve inches wide.

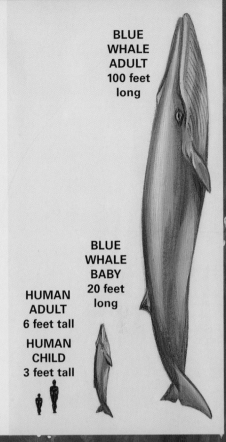

BLUE
WHALE
ADULT
100 feet
long

BLUE
WHALE
BABY
20 feet
long

HUMAN
ADULT
6 feet tall

HUMAN
CHILD
3 feet tall

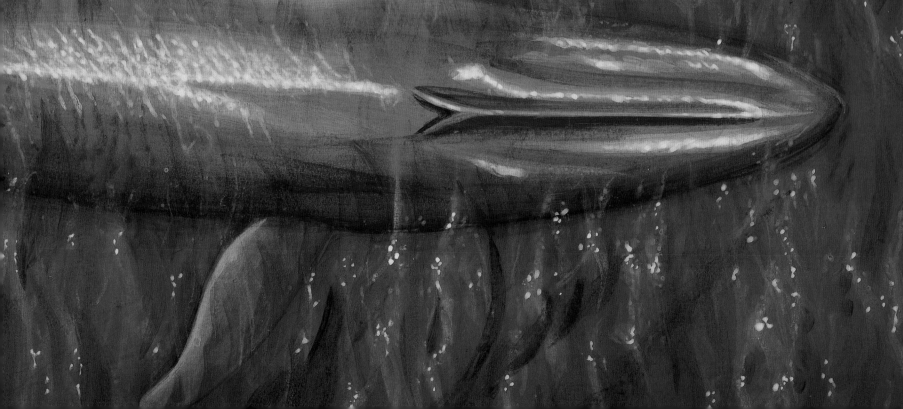

The giant panda mother gives birth to a very tiny baby. It weighs only about five ounces, about the same as a stick of butter. The mother weighs 700 times more than her baby. If your mother had weighed 700 times more than you when you were born, she would have been too big to fit inside your house!

At birth, a giant panda baby's pink skin is covered with hair. Its tiny belly button shows through the thin, white hair.

When baby monkeys and apes are born, their belly buttons show. But as they get older, hair grows out and hides their belly buttons.

The fur over an orangutan's belly button is much longer than the hair on the rest of its body.

Chimpanzee

Baboon

Gorilla

Underneath the hair on a gorilla's abdomen is a small belly button bump.

People's belly buttons are the easiest to see because we are not covered with fur.

Some people are "innies." Their belly buttons turn in. Some people are "outies." Their belly buttons stick out. Are you an "innie" or an "outie?"

You can think of your belly button as your birthday button. It marks your very first day of life outside your mother—the day you were born.

GLOSSARY

embryo
An unborn animal in the earliest stages of development.

fetus
An unborn mammal in the later stages of development. In humans, an embryo is called a fetus after it is eight weeks old.

mammal
A vertebrate, warm-blooded animal, usually with hair or fur on its skin. Female mammals, with the exception of the monotremes (platypuses and echidnas), give birth to living young and feed them with milk from their mammary glands.

mammary gland
Organs in the breasts of female mammals that produce milk for their young after birth.

navel
A spot on the abdomen of mammals that marks the place where the umbilic cord was attached.

oxygen
A colorless, odorless, tasteless gas. Animals, plants, and most other organisms need oxygen to live.

placenta
A special organ, composed of many blood vessels, that connects the embryo and then the fetus to the mother's uterus. The placenta sends oxygen and food materials through the umbilical cord to the fetus and receives wast materials from it.

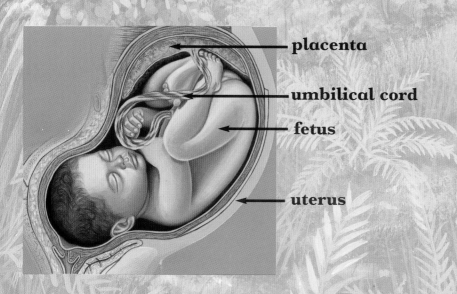

placenta

umbilical cord

fetus

uterus

umbilical cord
A long, tubelike structure that connects the developing embryo or fetus with the placenta in the uterus of a mammal mother. It contains blood vessels that carry blood containing oxygen and food materials to the fetus and carries waste products away from the fetus to the placenta.

uterus
The organ in most female mammals in which the embry and then the fetus develops. It is also called the womb.